ONCE UPON A BLUE MOOSE

THREE NOVELS

• • • • •

Blue Moose
Return of the Moose
The Moosepire

DANIEL PINKWATER

A YEARLING BOOK

To Jill, who was with me the time we met that moose
in the gas station in Greenville, Maine
• • • • •

Published by Yearling, an imprint of Random House Children's Books
a division of Random House, Inc., New York

Blue Moose was originally published in 1975 by Dodd, Mead & Co.
Return of the Blue Moose was originally published in 1979 by Dodd, Mead & Co.
The Moosepire was originally published in 1986 by Little, Brown & Company.

Yearling and the jumping horse design are registered trademarks of Random House, Inc.

Visit us on the Web! www.randomhouse.com/kids

Educators and librarians, for a variety of teaching tools, visit us at
www.randomhouse.com/teachers

ISBN: 0-440-42083-0
ISBN: 0-385-90308-1 (GLB)
Reprinted by arrangement with Alfred A. Knopf Books for Young Readers
Printed in the United States of America
March 2006
10 9 8 7 6 5 4 3 2 1

CONTENTS

• • • • •

The moose shines bright,
The stars give a light,
And you may kiss a porcupine
At ten o'clock at night.

• • • • •

Dear Reader,

I must warn you that the author of this book, Mr. Pinkwater, is a well-known ninny—and he is not very careful about keeping to the facts. There are many mistakes in this book—for example, Pinkwater does not tell you that all of Mr. Breton's recipes are really mine, and that I taught him to cook. Also, he never mentions what a handsome moose I am, nor does he tell how popular and famous I am.

I have always meant to write my own story, and someday I will do that. In the meantime, I hope you will enjoy these little tales of a moose, even though they are not perfect.

Your friend,
The Moose

BLUE MOOSE

MOOSE MEETING

MR. BRETON had a little restaurant on the edge of the big woods. There was nothing north of Mr. Breton's house except nothing, with trees in between. When winter came, the north wind blew through the trees and froze everything solid. Then it would snow. Mr. Breton didn't like it.

Mr. Breton was a very good cook. Every day, people from the town came to his restaurant. They ate gallons of his special clam chowder. They ate plates of his special beef stew. They ate fish stew and Mr. Breton's special homemade bread. The people from the town never talked much and they never said anything about his cooking.

"Did you like your clam chowder?" Mr. Breton would ask.

"Yup," the people from the town would say.

Mr. Breton wished they would say, "Delicious!" or, "Good chowder, Breton!" All they ever said was, "Yup." In winter they came on skis and snowshoes.

Every morning Mr. Breton went out behind his house to get firewood. He wore three sweaters, a scarf, galoshes, a woolen hat, a big checkered coat, and mittens. He still felt cold. Sometimes animals came out of the woods to watch Mr. Breton. Raccoons and rabbits came. The cold didn't bother them. It bothered Mr. Breton even more when they watched him.

One morning there was a moose in Mr. Breton's yard. It was a blue moose. When Mr. Breton went out his back door, the moose was there, looking at him. After a while, Mr. Breton went back in, closed the door, and made a pot of coffee while he waited for the moose to go away. It didn't go away; it just stood in Mr. Breton's yard, looking at his back door. Mr. Breton drank a cup of coffee. The moose stood in the yard. Mr. Breton opened the door again. "Shoo! Go away!" he said.

"Do you mind if I come in and get warm?" the moose said. "I'm just about frozen." The moose brushed past him and walked into the kitchen. His antlers almost touched the ceiling.

The moose sat down on the floor next to Mr. Breton's stove. He closed his eyes and sat leaning toward the stove for a long time. Mr. Breton stood in the kitchen, looking at the moose. The moose didn't move. Wisps of steam began to rise from his blue fur. After a long time the moose sighed. It sounded like a foghorn.

"Can I get you a cup of coffee?" Mr. Breton asked the moose. "Or some clam chowder?"

"Clam chowder," said the moose.

Mr. Breton filled a bowl with creamy clam chowder and set it on the floor. The moose dipped his big nose into the bowl and snuffled up the chowder. He made a sort of slurping, whistling noise.

"Sir," the moose said, "this is wonderful clam chowder."

Mr. Breton blushed a very deep red. "Do you really mean that?"

"Sir," the moose said, "I have eaten some very good chowder in my time, and yours is the very best."

"Oh my," said Mr. Breton, blushing even redder. "Oh my. Would you like some more?"

"Yes, with crackers," said the moose.

The moose ate seventeen bowls of chowder with crackers. Then he had twelve pieces of hot ginger-bread and forty-eight cups of coffee. While the moose slurped and whistled, Mr. Breton sat in a chair. Every now and then he said to himself, "Oh my. The best he's ever eaten. Oh my."

Later, when some people from the town came to Mr. Breton's house, the moose met them at the door. "How many in your party, please?" the moose asked. "I have a table for you; please follow me."

The people from the town were surprised to see the moose. They felt like running away, but they were too surprised. The moose led them to a table, brought them menus, looked at each person, snorted, and clumped into the kitchen.

"There are some people outside; I'll take care of them," he told Mr. Breton.

The people were whispering to one another about the moose, when he clumped back to the table.

"Are you ready to order?"

"Yup," the people from the town said. They waited for the moose to ask them if they would like some chowder, the way Mr. Breton always did. But the moose just stared at them as though they were very foolish. The people felt uncomfortable. "We'll have the clam chowder."

"Chaudière de Clam; very good," the moose said. "Do you desire crackers or homemade bread?"

"We will have crackers," said the people from the town.

"I suggest you have the bread; it is hot," said the moose.

"We will have bread," said the people from the town.

"And for dessert," said the moose, "will you have fresh gingerbread or Apple Jacquette?"

"What do you recommend?" asked the people from the town.

"After the Chaudière de Clam, the gingerbread is best."

"Thank you," said the people from the town.

"It is my pleasure to serve you," said the moose.

The moose brought bowls of chowder balanced on his antlers.

At the end of the meal, the moose clumped to the table. "Has everything been to your satisfaction?" he asked.

"Yup," said the people from the town, their mouths full of gingerbread.

"I beg your pardon?" said the moose. "What did you say?"

"It was very good," said the people from the town. "It was the best we've ever eaten."

"I will tell the chef," said the moose.

The moose clumped into the kitchen and told Mr. Breton that the people from the town had said that the food was the best they had ever eaten. Mr. Breton rushed out of the kitchen and out of the house. The people from the town were sitting on the porch, putting on their snowshoes.

"Did you tell the moose that my clam chowder was the best you've ever eaten?" Mr. Breton asked.

"Yup," said the people from the town, "we said that. We think that you are the best cook in the world; we have always thought so."

"Always?" asked Mr. Breton.

"Of course," the people from the town said.

"Why do you think we walk seven miles on snow-shoes just to eat here?"

The people from the town walked away on their snowshoes. Mr. Breton sat on the edge of the porch and thought it over. When the moose came out to see why Mr. Breton was sitting outside without his coat on, Mr. Breton said, "Do you know, those people think I am the best cook in the whole world?"

"Of course they do," the moose said. "Do you want me to go into town to get some crackers? We seem to have run out."

"Yes," said Mr. Breton, "and get some asparagus too. I'm going to cook something special tomorrow."

"By the way," said the moose, "aren't you cold out here?"

"No, I'm not the least bit cold," Mr. Breton said. "This is turning out to be a very mild winter."

GAME WARDEN

THERE WAS a lot of talk in town about the moose at Mr. Breton's restaurant. Some people who had never been there before went to the restaurant just to see the moose. There was an article in the newspaper about the moose, and how he talked to the customers, and brought them their bowls of clam chowder, and helped Mr. Breton in the kitchen.

Some people from other towns drove a long way with chains on their tires to Mr. Breton's restaurant, just to see the moose. Mr. Breton was always very busy waiting on tables at lunchtime and suppertime.

The moose was always very polite to the people,

but he made them feel a little uncomfortable too. He looked at people with only one eye at a time, and he was better than most of them at pronouncing French words. He knew what kind of wine to drink with clam chowder, and he knew which kind of wine to drink with the special beef stew. Some of the people in the town bragged that the moose was a friend of theirs, and always gave them a table right away. When they came to the restaurant they would pat the moose on the back, and say, "Hello, Moose, you remember me, don't you?"

"There will be a slight delay until a table is ready," the moose would say, and snort, and shake himself.

Mr. Breton was very happy in the kitchen. There were pots of all sorts of good things steaming on the stove and smelling good, and bread baking in the oven from morning to night. Mr. Breton loved to cook good things for lots of people, the more the better. He had never been so busy and happy in his life.

One morning, Mr. Bobowicz, the game warden, came to the restaurant. "Mr. Breton, are you aware of Section 5—Subheading 6—Paragraph 3

of the state fish and game laws?" said Mr. Bobowicz.

"No, I am not aware of Section 5—Subheading 6—Paragraph 3," Mr. Breton said. "What is it all about?"

"No person shall keep a moose as a pet, tie up a moose, keep a moose in a pen or barn, or parlor or bedroom, or any such enclosure," said Mr. Bobowicz. "In short, it is against the law to have a tame moose."

"Oh my," said Mr. Breton, "I don't want to do anything against the law. But I don't keep the moose. He just came along one day, and has stayed ever since. He helps me run my restaurant."

Mr. Bobowicz rubbed his chin. "And where is the aforesaid moose?"

Mr. Breton had given the moose one of the rooms upstairs, in which there was a particularly large bed. The moose just fit in the bed, if he folded up his feet. He liked it very much; he said he never had a bed of his own. The moose slept on the bed under six blankets, and during the day he would go upstairs sometimes, and stretch out on the bed and sigh with pleasure.

When Mr. Bobowicz came to see Mr. Breton, the moose had been downstairs to help Mr. Breton eat a giant breakfast, and then he had wandered back to his room to enjoy lying on his bed until the lunchtime customers arrived. He heard Mr. Breton and Mr. Bobowicz talking. The moose bugled. He had never bugled in Mr. Breton's house before. Bugling is a noise that no animal except a moose can really do right. Elk can bugle, and elephants can bugle, and some kinds of geese and swans can bugle, but it is nothing like moose bugling. When the moose bugled, the whole house jumped and rattled, dishes clinked together in the cupboard, pots and pans clanged together, icicles fell off the house.

"I AM NOT A TAME MOOSE!" the moose shouted from where he was lying on his bed.

Mr. Bobowicz looked at Mr. Breton with very wide eyes. "Was that the moose?"

The moose had gotten out of bed, and was clumping down the stairs. "You're flipping right, that was the moose," he growled.

The moose clumped right up to Mr. Bobowicz, and looked at him with one red eye. The moose's

nose was touching Mr. Bobowicz's nose. They just stood there, looking at each other, for a long time. The moose was breathing loudly, and his eye seemed to be a glowing coal. Mr. Bobowicz's knees were shaking. Then the moose spoke very slowly. "You . . . are . . . a . . . tame . . . game warden."

The moose turned, and clumped back up the stairs. Mr. Breton and Mr. Bobowicz heard him sigh and heard the springs crash and groan as he flopped onto the big bed.

"Mr. Bobowicz, the moose is not tame," Mr. Breton said. "He is a wild moose, and he lives here of his own free will; he is the headwaiter." Mr. Breton spoke very quietly, because Mr. Bobowicz had not moved since the moose had come down-stairs. His eyes were still open very wide, and his knees were still shaking. Mr. Breton took Mr. Bobowicz by the hand, and led him into the kitchen and poured him a cup of coffee.

DAVE

NOT VERY FAR from Mr. Breton's house, in a secret place in the woods, lived a hermit named Dave. Everybody knew that Dave was out there, but nobody ever saw him. Mr. Bobowicz, the game warden, had seen what might have been Dave a couple of times; or it might have been a shadow. Sometimes, late at night, Mr. Breton would hear the wind whistling strangely, and think of Dave.

The moose brought Dave home with him one night. They were old friends. Dave was dressed in rabbit skins, stitched together. His feet were wrapped in tree bark and moose-moss. An owl sat on his head.

"Dave is very shy," the moose said. "He would appreciate it if you didn't say anything to him until he knows you better, maybe in ten or fifteen years. He knows about your gingerbread, and he would like to try it." While the moose spoke, Dave blushed very red, and tried to cover his face with the owl, which fluttered and squawked.

Mr. Breton put dishes with gingerbread and applesauce and fresh whipped cream in front of Dave, the moose, and the owl. There was no noise but the moose slurping, and Dave's spoon scraping. Mr. Breton turned to get the coffeepot. When he looked back at the table, Dave and the owl were gone.

"Dave says thank you," the moose said.

The next night Dave was back, and this time he had a whistle made out of a turkey bone in his hat. After the gingerbread, Dave played on the whistle, like the wind making strange sounds; the moose hummed, and Mr. Breton clicked two spoons, while the owl hopped up and down on the kitchen table, far into the night.

HUMS
OF A MOOSE

ONE DAY, after the moose had been staying with Mr. Breton for a fairly long time, there was an especially heavy snowfall. The snow got to be as high as the house, and there was no way for people to come from the town.

Mr. Breton got a big fire going in the stove, and kept adding pieces of wood until the stove was glowing red. The house was warm, and filled with the smell of applesauce, which Mr. Breton was cooking in big pots on the stove. Mr. Breton was peeling apples and the moose was sitting on the floor, lapping every now and then at a big chowder bowl full of coffee on the kitchen table.

The moose didn't say anything. Mr. Breton didn't say anything. Now and then the moose would take a deep breath with his nose in the air, sniffing in the smell of apples and cinnamon and raisins cooking. Then he would sigh. The sighs got louder and longer.

The moose began to hum—softly, then louder. The humming made the table shake, and Mr. Breton felt the humming in his fingers each time he picked up an apple. The humming mixed with the apple and cinnamon smell and melted the frost on the windows, and the room filled with sunlight. Mr. Breton smelled flowers.

Then he could see them. The kitchen floor had turned into a meadow with new grass, dandelions, periwinkles, and daisies.

The moose hummed. Mr. Breton smelled melting snow. He heard ice cracking. He felt the ground shake under the hoofs of moose returning from the low, wet places. Rabbits bounded through the fields. Bears, thin after the winter's sleep, came out of hiding. Birds sang.

The people in the town could not remember such an unseasonable thaw. The weather got

warm all of a sudden, and the ice and snow melted for four days before winter set in again. When they went to Mr. Breton's restaurant, they discovered that he had made a wonderful stew with lots of carrots that reminded them of meadows in springtime.

MOOSE
MOVING

WHEN SPRING finally came, the moose became moody. He spent a lot of time staring out the back door. Flocks of geese flew overhead, returning to lakes in the North, and the moose always stirred when he heard their honking.

"Chef," the moose said one morning, "I will be going tomorrow. I wonder if you would pack some gingerbread for me to take along."

Mr. Breton baked a special batch of gingerbread, and packed it in parcels tied with string, so the moose could hang them from his antlers. When the moose came downstairs, Mr. Breton was sitting in

the kitchen drinking coffee. The parcels of gingerbread were on the kitchen table.

"Do you want a bowl of coffee before you go?"
Mr. Breton asked.

"Thank you," said the moose.

"I shall certainly miss you," Mr. Breton said.

"Thank you," said the moose.

"You are the best friend I have," said Mr. Breton.

"Thank you," said the moose.

"Do you suppose you'll ever come back?" Mr.
Breton asked.

"Not before Thursday or Friday," said the moose.
"It would be impolite to visit my uncle for less
than a week."

The moose hooked his antlers into the loops of
string on the packages of gingerbread. "My uncle
will like this." He stood up and turned to the
door.

"Wait!" Mr. Breton shouted. "Do you mean that
you are not leaving forever? I thought you were
lonely for the life of a wild moose. I thought you
wanted to go back to the wild, free places."

"Chef, do you have any idea how cold it gets in

the wild, free places?" the moose said. "And the food! Terrible!"

"Have a nice time at your uncle's," said Mr. Breton.

"I'll send you a postcard," said the moose.

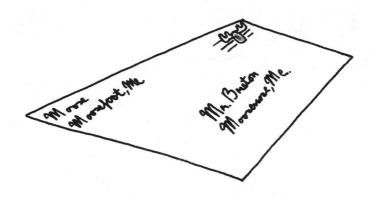

MOOSE QUESTIONS AND ANTLERS

What is a moose?

Moose are the largest member of the deer family. They can be found in Alaska, Canada, and northern parts of the United States, as well as northern Europe and Asia, and at least one moose in recent years wandered into the northern part of New York City. Moose are herbivores, meaning plant-eaters. They can weigh up to 1,500 pounds. They vary in size and shape, like everybody else. They can be anywhere from light brown to almost black.

The moose has a long nose, a drooping lip, a hump at the shoulders, a small tail, and a dangling flap of skin at the throat, called a bell. Other moose think this is a very handsome arrangement. The height of a moose at the shoulder ranges between six and a half and seven and a half feet. Only the males grow antlers, which can have as many as thirty "tines," or spikes. Mature moose shed their antlers every year in November or December, and grow new ones. The purpose of the antlers is to impress other moose.

Can you ride a moose?

In the eighteenth century, the Swedish cavalry experimented with moose as mounts for soldiers. They found that moose are stronger and more durable than horses, and aré more agile than horses in more kinds of terrain. The Swedes were able to train the moose, and ride them, but they couldn't keep the moose from running away from gunfire. So, moose are obviously smarter than horses.

Can you milk a moose?

People in Sweden seem to be unable to stop trying to find practical uses for moose, and some farmers there milk moose cows. It takes up to two hours to milk a moose. (I don't know if that includes catching an animal that can run at fifty-five miles per hour.)

Each moose cow produces only one gallon of milk per day. However, moose-milk cheese sells for five hundred dollars a pound. I have never tasted any moose-milk cheese, but I would like to—if somebody else paid for it.

RETURN OF THE MOOSE

1

FOR A LONG time, the blue moose had been help-ing Mr. Breton run his restaurant on the edge of the big woods. The moose had turned up one win-ter day, and gone to work as the headwaiter. Actually, he was the only waiter. Mr. Breton did the cooking, and the moose took care of the cus-tomers. Mr. Breton liked the arrangement. He had been lonely before the blue moose came, and the customers were much more polite to the moose than they had been to Mr. Breton. It's not easy to be impolite to an animal over eight feet tall.

Mr. Breton and the moose were friends, but they didn't talk very much. The moose did his work,

Mr. Breton did his work, and the people who came to eat in the restaurant were satisfied. Late in the evening, when all the cleaning up had been done, Mr. Breton and the moose would sit together, and drink coffee. Mr. Breton drank his coffee from a cup. The blue moose drank coffee from a soup bowl. Sometimes the moose would help Mr. Breton in the kitchen, and they would sing together. The moose didn't sing so much as hum. He had a very nice humming voice.

On Sundays, and between mealtimes, when there was no one in the restaurant, the blue moose would go for long walks in the woods and meadows, or sit in his room upstairs. Sometimes, the moose would take a vacation, and go off to visit moose friends or relatives.

The moose never talked about his life before he came to the restaurant, and Mr. Breton was too polite to ask questions. Mr. Breton never talked about his life before he opened the restaurant, because opening the restaurant was the second most interesting thing that had ever happened to him. The first most interesting thing that had ever happened to Mr. Breton was when the blue moose came to help him.

Sometimes friends dropped by. Mr. Bobowicz, the game warden, would come to visit, and Dave, a hermit who lived in the woods, liked to come late at night with his pet owl. When friends came, they would sit in the kitchen with Mr. Breton and the blue moose, and drink coffee, and eat hot gingerbread. Sometimes they would sing.

When Mr. Breton and the moose talked, they would usually discuss business matters having to do with the restaurant.

"Chef," the moose would say, "when I go into town tomorrow for supplies, do you want me to get some parsnips? We're almost out of parsnips."

"Yes," Mr. Breton would say, "and if you can find some very nice turnips, get those too. I'm thinking about experimenting with turnips in my beef stew."

"That's a very good idea, Chef," the moose would say.

"Thank you," Mr. Breton would say. "I spent all day Wednesday thinking about it."

"It is an inspiration, Chef," the moose would say.

"Thank you very much," Mr. Breton would say.

One day, the moose said to Mr. Breton, "Chef, in the basement of this restaurant, I noticed an old typewriter. Would it be all right if I kept it in my room?"

"Of course," Mr. Breton said. Then he said, "I hope you don't mind my asking. I hope you don't think I'm impolite. But what does a moose want with a typewriter?"

"I'm going to type with it, Chef," said the moose.

"Oh," said Mr. Breton.

THE NEXT morning, when Mr. Breton was preparing things in the kitchen, at the time when the moose usually stayed in bed, Mr. Breton heard the clicking of a typewriter from the moose's room. The moose typed slowly, one click at a time. He kept it up for more than an hour.

At the time when the moose usually came downstairs for his soup bowl of coffee and fifteen or twenty pieces of gingerbread, he was still clicking away on the typewriter. Mr. Breton put the soup bowl of coffee and fifteen or twenty pieces of gingerbread on a tray and carried it upstairs. He knocked softly on the door of the moose's room.

"Come in," said the blue moose.

Mr. Breton went in. The moose was sitting in bed with the typewriter balanced on his knees. Surrounding him were stacks of paper with writing in longhoof. There was also a pile of neatly typed pages. The moose was reading from the sheets of paper written in longhoof, and typing what he read.

"I hope my typing does not disturb you," said the moose. "If it bothers you while you are cooking, I could type at another time."

"No, no, not at all," Mr. Breton said. "I like the sound of the typing. It reminds me of drops of rain falling on the roof. I just thought you might like it if I brought your coffee and gingerbread to you."

"Thank you," said the moose. "That was most considerate."

"I don't suppose you'd want to tell me what you are writing," Mr. Breton said.

"Not at this time," said the moose.

From that time on, every morning, the moose typed in his room while Mr. Breton worked in the kitchen. Every morning, Mr. Breton brought a soup bowl of coffee and fifteen or twenty pieces of gingerbread to the moose. Every morning, Mr. Breton said, "How is it going today?"

"Just fine," the moose would say.

"I don't suppose you'd want to tell me what you are writing," Mr. Breton would say.

"Not at this time," the moose would say.

Mr. Breton would go back to the kitchen. For a while there would be no sound of typing, as the moose slurped up his soup bowl of coffee and ate his fifteen or twenty pieces of gingerbread. Then the clicking would start again, reminding Mr. Breton of drops of rain falling on the roof.

Mr. Breton was very curious about what the blue moose was writing, but whenever he asked the moose, the moose would say, "Not at this time."

3

ONE MORNING when Mr. Breton came down to begin work in the kitchen, he found the blue moose standing and staring out of the kitchen window.

"You're up early," Mr. Breton said.

The moose said nothing.

"No typing this morning?" Mr. Breton said.

The moose said nothing.

"Coffee?" Mr. Breton said.

The moose said nothing.

"You're not mad at me, are you?" Mr. Breton said.

The moose said nothing.

Mr. Breton set about making a big pot of coffee. When it was ready, he said, "Moose, come and have some coffee."

The moose sighed. When a moose sighs, it is always very expressive. This sigh was even more expressive than usual. It made the dishes in the cupboards rattle and clatter. It made the windows and the stovepipe rattle and buzz. It made two flies, who had been circling near the ceiling, stop, listen, forget to move their wings, and fall to the floor. It made little ripples in the coffee in Mr. Breton's cup, and in the soup bowl he had filled for the moose.

"Something bothering you?" Mr. Breton asked.

The moose sighed again. The dishes rattled, the windows and stovepipe buzzed. The two flies looked at each other, and began crawling toward the kitchen door. Little waves appeared on the surface of the coffee.

"Oh, an artist's life is hard, Chef—hard, hard, hard," the blue moose said.

"Yes, I suppose it is," Mr. Breton said. "Is that why you were sighing?"

"My work, my life, my masterpiece!" the moose

said. "Everything has gone sour! It seemed to be going so well, and now . . . disaster!"

"Does this have something to do with all the typing you've been doing?" Mr. Breton asked.

"Oh, why, *why*, WHY am I punished like this?" the moose moaned. Then he clumped upstairs. Mr. Breton heard the bedsprings crash and groan as the moose hurled himself into bed.

That day the moose did not come downstairs to help Mr. Breton. Mr. Breton had to do all the cooking, and wait on the customers. The moose stayed in his bed all day, with a newspaper over his head.

Every now and then, when things weren't too busy in the restaurant, Mr. Breton would go upstairs and peek into the moose's room. The blue moose sat in his bed, with the newspaper covering his head, and said nothing.

After the last customer had gone, Mr. Breton brought the moose a big bowl of beef stew with turnips.

"Leave it on the table," the moose said.

The moose stayed in bed, with the newspaper over his head, for five days. Mr. Bobowicz, the game warden, and Dave, the hermit, came to visit the moose, but he wouldn't talk to them. He just sat in bed, with a newspaper covering his head. Every now and then the moose would sigh, and frighten the customers in the restaurant.

Mr. Breton was worried about the moose. At night, he would sit in a chair beside the moose's bed, but the moose wouldn't talk to him.

4

ON THE SIXTH day, when Mr. Breton went down to the kitchen to begin his work, he heard the moose typing in his room. Mr. Breton smiled. He made a big pot of coffee, and a fresh batch of gingerbread. When the gingerbread was ready, he poured applesauce all over it. The moose liked it that way. He put twenty-five pieces of gingerbread on a tray, and went up to the moose's room.

"Good morning, Chef," the moose said. "It's a beautiful morning, isn't it? I see you've brought me some gingerbread. How thoughtful! Thank you, Chef, ever so much."

"I guess things are going better with whatever it is you've been writing," Mr. Breton said.

"My book?" said the moose. "My masterpiece? My work of literature? It couldn't be better. I'll have it finished this afternoon."

"Oh, it's a book you've been writing," Mr. Breton said.

"Not just a book," said the blue moose. "Not just any book—it is a great book, the most wonderful book ever written by man or moose. I'll admit I had a bit of trouble with it for a while, but that's all behind me now. This will be the greatest book anybody has ever seen . . . the greatest book ever written—and, Chef, I wonder if you'd do me a favor . . ."

"Of course," said Mr. Breton.

"I'd like you to be the first person to read my book," the blue moose said.

"It would be an honor," said Mr. Breton.

"Tonight after the restaurant closes," said the moose.

That night, after Mr. Breton had finished his work, the moose went upstairs to get his book. Mr. Breton cleared the big table in the kitchen, and poured a cup of coffee for himself, and a soup bowl of coffee for the moose. Mr. Breton put on his reading glasses, took them off, cleaned them with the tail of his shirt, put them on again, took them off again, cleaned them some more, put them on again, and sat down to wait for the moose.

The moose brought down the book he had written and put it on the kitchen table in front of Mr. Breton. He had also drawn some pictures to go with the book, and they were tucked in, here and there, between the typed pages.

Mr. Breton began to read. The moose paced up and down in the kitchen. "How do you like it so far?" the moose asked him.

"I've just begun to read the first sentence," Mr. Breton said.

Mr. Breton continued to read. "Oh my!" he said.

"What? What?" the moose said. "What part are you reading now?"

"I was just going to say . . ." Mr. Breton said. "Oh my! I can't read with you pacing up and down like that. Now sit down and drink your coffee while I read your book."

The moose sat down. Mr. Breton read. This is the book that Mr. Breton read. This is the book the moose had written, the book that Mr. Breton read at the kitchen table, in the evening, after the restaurant had closed.

5

THE TRUE STORY OF A WILD MOOSE
by D. Moosus Moosewater

After single-handedly defeating Nazi Germany
and Imperial Japan, and thus ending World War
II, I decided to devote myself to finding a cure for
all diseases known to Man and Moose. However,
before I was able to do this, I found that my country still needed me to serve as President of the
United States. In those days, I was known by the
name of Harry S. Truman.

While being President was a great honor, I found
the job boring. The only parts I liked were my

PRESIDENT

vacations. During one vacation, I set the world's record for holding my breath under water—two hours and forty-three minutes. I also set the still-unbroken world records for the high jump, the hundred-yard dash, and the mile. Due to a technicality, my records were not official. It turned out that four-footed creatures are not allowed to compete, so my name is not in the record books. I was disappointed, and I gave up sports.

On another vacation, I discovered the largest gold mine on earth, under a vacant lot in Bayonne, New Jersey, and gave it as a present to the United States. But my favorite vacation was the one during which I became the first moose to climb Mount Everest. I climbed it three times. I could have climbed it more, but on the third day of my vacation, I received an urgent message to come back to the White House.

After I got through being President of the United States, I decided to devote some time to space travel, so I designed and built all the rockets and space vehicles which would be used later to carry men to the Moon. I had already had a lot of experience inventing things. I had already

invented the jet airplane, color television, computers, and the cheeseburger.

Of all my great adventures, the most exciting, and the one that presented the greatest danger to Earth, was the invasion of the Moose from Space. At the time this happened, I was busy carving the heads of Washington, Jefferson, Lincoln, and Teddy Roosevelt on Mount Rushmore. A message was brought to me that a spaceship had landed in Washington, D.C., not far from the Capitol. Out of the spaceship had come a gigantic moose, more than fifty feet high. The moose refused to move. He just stood there, demanding that the President of the United States, and all the presidents and kings on Earth, assemble outside his spaceship no later than the following Tuesday.

Fearing that the Moose from Space had hostile intentions, the army and police had shot him, bombed him, set fire to him, set dynamite off under him, set vicious dogs after him, squirted him with insect spray, and thrown big rocks at him. None of this had the slightest effect on the Moose from Space. He did seem less friendly after all

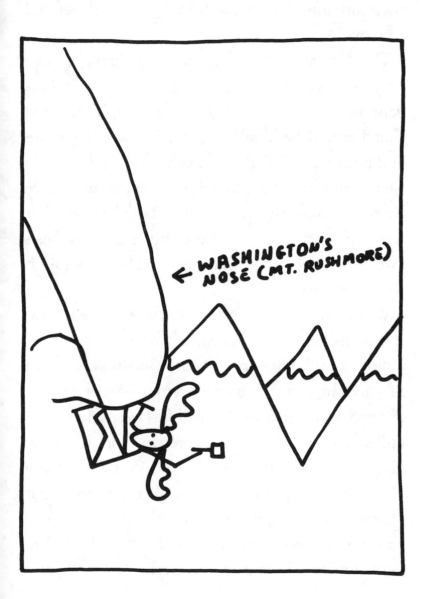

these attempts to subdue him, but he still refused to move.

The last resort for the people of Earth was to send for me, the strongest, bravest, most intelligent moose in the world. Some people doubted that I would be able to succeed where dynamite and bombs had failed, and even I was slightly worried. After all, the Moose from Space was more than six times my size, and nobody knew what secret powers he might have. But I did not hesitate. An Army plane was sent to take me straight to Washington, D.C.

When I saw the space moose, I was amazed. I was astounded. I was shocked. I was shaken. I was almost afraid. The space moose was every bit of fifty feet high. He had an enormous set of antlers. His eyes were red and glowed like twenty-five-watt bulbs. He had a nasty expression on his face. Human people can't usually tell if a moose has a pleasant expression or an unpleasant one—but another moose can tell. This moose was an ugly customer if I ever saw one. I knew that if I had to fight him, it was going to be a terrible battle. Not

only was he strong, but I could tell he was sneaky. He might pull a knife or anything.

The best approach to a moose like that is not to let him know that you are afraid. I marched right up to him. "What do you want here, you big palooka?" I asked him.

The space moose sneered an ugly sneer. "Go away, sonny, you bother me," he said.

He was trying to get me mad. I knew that if I made a rash move, the space moose would thump me with his antlers, which probably weighed a ton. I remained cool. "Where I come from," I said, "the people eat moose of your size in sandwiches, horns and all. Now tell me what you want before I get ugly."

No moose on Earth likes to have his antlers referred to as "horns," and apparently space moose are just the same. The big moose began to breathe hard through his nose. "If you're a moose," he said, "and not a mouse—which you might be, judging from your size—you should know better than to talk that way."

"I'm a moose all right," I said, "and what are you? You look like a great big dairy cow to me."

"You're about to get into trouble, peewee," the space moose said.

The space moose was getting really mad now. That was what I wanted. If I had to fight him, I wanted him to make some foolish moves. "I'm tired of all this social chatter," I said. "Now tell me what you're doing here before I call the farmer who takes care of you."

That did it. The space moose was in a perfect rage. "I'll tell you," he snorted, "before I trample you into a moose-flavored pizza, I'll tell you exactly what I'm doing here." The space moose was so angry now that he couldn't stand still. He was so angry that his ears were actually spinning like the propellers on an airplane. "What I'm doing here, you miserable pip-squeak," the space moose said, "what I'm doing here is waiting for the people of Earth to surrender no later than next Tuesday. I come from a planet in the galaxy of Betelmoose, where all the inhabitants are big, tough moose like me. Every now and then, we take over a planet, and push everybody around, and destroy things just for fun. I'm the biggest, toughest moose, so they send me down first to make everybody surrender. Then, I call the other moose on the radio, and they all come down here, and we have a good time. And we don't leave until the place is a real mess. But right now, I'm going to make mooseburger out of you."

"Wait a minute while I tie one hoof behind my back," I said.

The space moose made a dive for me with his antlers. I made a deft move to the side, and he missed me. Then he reared up and tried to get me with his hooves. I dodged out of the way, and bit him on the rump for good measure. That made him even madder, and he began striking out in every direction. His punches were wild. He never touched me. Every now and then, I'd see a chance, and poke him—with my hoof, with my antlers— thrust and parry—turn and thrust—butt and kick. The space moose was confused. He didn't know where he was. I was in complete control of the fight—but the space moose never got tired. One- sixth his size, I had to do a lot of moving to keep out of the way of his punishing hooves and antlers. I saw that I'd have to find some way to finish the fight before I started to get tired myself. In the

course of our battle, we had covered a lot of distance. I realized that we had fought our way over to the Washington Monument. I managed to move around so that the Washington Monument was behind me. Then I pretended to be tired. I stopped moving and just stood there, pretending to be trying to get my breath. The space moose stopped too. This was what he was waiting for. He was slower but stronger. He knew that when I got tired, I would be at his mercy.

The space moose took a couple of steps backward. He was getting ready to charge. I pretended to be too tired to move out of the way. Then he put his head down, and ran at me. At the last moment, I jumped about fifteen feet to one side. His antlers were so wide that he just missed me by inches as he crashed directly into the base of the Washington Monument. He staggered backward, still on his feet. The force of the impact broke off the top sixty or seventy feet of the monument, which fell in one piece, and bounced off his head. He sat down, dazed.

The space moose shook his head. "How did you do that?" he asked.

"Never mind, bozo," I said. "Just get into your little airplane and fly off before I lose my temper."

The space moose staggered off and got into his spaceship, and lifted off. I received a platinum medal, and a check for fifty billion dollars from a grateful Earth. The Washington Monument was repaired, of course. I did it free of charge.

And that is how I saved Earth from the space moose invaders and had my greatest adventure.

THE END

"Well," said the blue moose, "how did you like it?"

"It's very exciting," Mr. Breton said. "Is any of it true?"

"Humph!" snorted the moose, and gathered up his pages and pictures, and went upstairs.

6

THE NEXT morning, the blue moose went into town with a big, flat package, wrapped in brown paper and tied with string. It was his book. He told Mr. Breton that he was mailing it to a publishing house, Klotz, Yold & Company, Inc.

"Do you think they'll publish it?" Mr. Breton asked.

"Chef, you amaze me," the moose said. "You read it, didn't you? It is a masterpiece. Not only will Klotz, Yold & Company, Inc. publish it, but it will make me rich and famous."

"Do you really think so?" Mr. Breton asked.

"Chef, you know a great deal about cooking,"

said the moose, "but apparently you know absolutely nothing about literature. Do I really think so? What a question! Klotz, Yold & Company, Inc. will shed tears of joy when they read my book. You'll see."

Then the moose sat down at the kitchen table, and looked out the window with a dreamy expression. Mr. Breton could tell that the moose was thinking about the days to come, when Klotz, Yold & Company, Inc. would publish his book, and he would become rich and famous.

For several weeks, the moose was very little help around the restaurant. He seemed to be unable to pay attention to his work. He would bring customers things they had not ordered, and not bring them things they had ordered. He would bring them their dessert at the beginning of the meal, and he would bring them their soup at the end of the meal. Several times, when the customers handed their menus to the moose, after looking at them, the moose would sign his autograph on the menus, and hand them back to the customers.

None of the customers complained about the moose's strange behavior. After all, who wants to argue with a moose? But Mr. Breton noticed it. He knew what was causing it. He knew that the moose was waiting to hear from Klotz, Yold & Company, Inc. Weeks went by.

The blue moose never gave up expecting that Klotz, Yold & Company, Inc. would want to publish his book. Once, Mr. Breton tried to bring up the subject. He tried to suggest the possibility that Klotz, Yold & Company, Inc. might, for whatever reasons, not want to publish the moose's book. "Nonsense," the moose said.

Mr. Breton was starting to worry about the moose. He was worried that Klotz, Yold & Company, Inc. might turn the book down, and make the moose very unhappy. In fact, he thought that Klotz, Yold & Company, Inc. *would* turn the book down. Mr. Breton thought it wasn't a very good book.

He talked to Mr. Bobowicz, the game warden, about it. "The moose has written a book," Mr. Breton said. "It is all about how he won World War Two, and was President of the United States, and climbed Mount Everest, and found a gold mine, and invented color television, and the cheeseburger. He says, in his book, that he fought a fifty-foot-tall moose from outer space. There isn't a single word of truth in it. Now he's sent it off to a publisher, and he's sure they will want to publish it, and make him rich and famous. Of course, the publisher will know that the book isn't true, and refuse to publish it. The moose will be so disappointed. I'm worried about him."

The next day, the moose received a letter from Klotz, Yold & Company, Inc., saying that they wanted to publish his book, and would he come to New York and talk with them about it.

7

MR. BRETON and Mr. Bobowicz, the game warden, saw the blue moose off at the train. Dave, the hermit, didn't actually come to the train, but they knew he was hiding in the trees at the edge of the tracks. Mr. Breton had packed sandwiches and a lot of gingerbread for the moose to eat on the trip. They all waved good-bye until the train was out of sight.

"I knew it!" Mr. Breton said to Mr. Bobowicz. "I knew the blue moose was going to be famous!"

The following day, the moose came back. He had presents for everybody. He gave Mr. Breton a real French chef's spoon. He gave Mr. Bobowicz a

whistle with a compass built in. He gave Dave a little notebook covered in red leather (Dave liked to make up poems), and a pencil that wrote in different colors.

For himself, the moose had bought a pair of eyeglasses, without any glass in them, and a pipe. He also gave Mr. Breton, Mr. Bobowicz, and Dave copies of a photograph of himself, wearing his eyeglasses and smoking his pipe. Klotz, Yold & Company, Inc., the publishers, had taken the picture to print on the back of the moose's book.

Mr. Breton was very proud of the moose. "How did it go?" he asked the moose.

"I signed a contract," the moose said. "They're going to print my book. They say that they may have to edit it a little—sort of fix up little parts, here and there—but they like it very much."

A long time passed. Mr. Breton could hardly wait for the moose's book to be published. The moose couldn't wait at all. He went out to look for the mail every five or ten minutes. In between, he practiced signing his autograph. The moose spent a lot of time looking at the photograph of himself wearing his eyeglasses and smoking his pipe.

One day a package arrived. It was from Klotz, Yold & Company, Inc. The moose was so excited that he couldn't unwrap it. Mr. Breton had to help him. "It's my book! It's my book!" the moose kept repeating. "It's *The True Story of a Wild Moose!*"

Mr. Breton unwrapped the book. On the cover was a picture of a lady moose wearing lipstick and long eyelashes. Over the picture of the lady moose was printing: "Hot Mooselove!" it said. There was more printing—

She was a sweet unspoiled moosegirl
until she met
THE MOOSE FROM SPACE!!!
An exciting love story!

Nowhere on the cover of the book did it say *The True Story of a Wild Moose*. For a moment, Mr. Breton and the moose thought that maybe it wasn't the blue moose's book. They thought that maybe it was some other book—but there on the back of the book was the picture of the moose wearing his eyeglasses and smoking his pipe.

The moose roared. It was a terrible roar. It broke

fifteen plates, two windows, and a cast-iron frying pan. "This is not my book!" the moose shouted. "There is no moosegirl in my book! There is no love story in my book! They changed everything! They said they were going to fix it up here and there—and they've changed everything!" Then the blue moose roared again, causing the paint to peel off the ceiling, and curdling twenty-six quarts of milk in the icebox—and rushed out of the kitchen, out of the restaurant, and out of sight.

8

THE BLUE MOOSE went missing. He was gone for two days. Mr. Breton closed the restaurant. He and Mr. Bobowicz, the game warden, and Dave, the hermit, spent all day looking for the moose. At night, they went out with flashlights. Mr. Bobowicz kept blowing the whistle the moose had given him. They didn't find him.

At last, the three men came back to the restaurant. They sat in the kitchen. Every so often, one of them would say, "Where can he be?"

The moose walked in. "Chef, can you fix me something for an upset stomach?" he said. "I've eaten six thousand copies of *The Moose from Space* and two electric typewriters, and I'm feeling just a little bit ill."

Mr. Breton, Mr. Bobowicz, the game warden, and Dave, the hermit, all jumped up and began talking at once.

"Where have you been?"

"Why did you run off like that?"

"We were all worried!"

Mr. Breton prepared a glass of fizzy stuff for the moose's upset stomach, and the blue moose drank it. "Another," he said.

"Moose," Mr. Breton said, as he prepared another glass of fizzy stuff, "please tell us where you've been."

"I've been to New York City," the moose said. "I've been to the book warehouse of Klotz, Yold & Company, Inc. That's where I ate all six thousand copies of that monstrosity they made out of my book. Then I went to the offices of Klotz, Yold & Company, Inc., and had a little talk with the people there. I explained to them that I wanted them to print my book, just the way it was written. That's where I ate the two electric typewriters. It wasn't that I was hungry—I just wanted to demonstrate to them that I am a very serious moose. They saw it my way, and they are going to print *The True Story of a Wild Moose*, just the way I wrote it."

"My goodness," Mr. Breton said.

"Yes, well, business can be very tiring," said the blue moose. "If you'll all excuse me, I think I'll go to bed now."

9

A WEEK LATER, Klotz, Yold & Company, Inc. sent the blue moose a copy of his book. On the cover was a picture of the fight between the moose and the space moose. "That's better," said the blue moose.

The book was a big success. Soon, the moose began getting letters every day. People asked him to come to schools and libraries and talk to audiences. Newspapers and magazines printed stories about the moose. The moose started to appear on television.

Mr. Breton bought a television set so he could watch the moose. Mr. Bobowicz, the game warden,

and Dave, the hermit, would come to Mr. Breton's restaurant in the evening, and they would sit together, eating popcorn, and watching the blue moose. Every time the moose was interviewed, he would remember to say, "By the way, the best food in the world is served at Mr. Breton's restaurant, and my friend, Mr. Breton, is the best chef in the world."

Although he appreciated the compliment, Mr. Breton wished the moose wouldn't say that. It was hard for him to take care of all the people who had come to eat in his restaurant since the moose had become famous—especially without the moose there to help him.

The moose was away, giving interviews, and talking to people, more than he was at home. Mr. Breton was happy for his friend. He was glad that his book was a big success, and that he was famous—but he missed the days when the moose was always there. He missed the days when he and the moose would run the restaurant together, quietly, not talking much.

Then Klotz, Yold & Company, Inc. wrote to the moose to say that a movie was going to be made of

The True Story of a Wild Moose, and that he, the moose, was wanted in Hollywood.

Mr. Breton gave a good-bye party for the blue moose. He made a special carrot cake. Mr. Bobowicz, the game warden, was there, and Dave, the hermit. The moose's friends tried to make it a happy party, but they were all sad to think that their friend was going so far away.

The moose went to Hollywood. He sent picture postcards to Mr. Breton. Once, Mr. Breton saw the moose on a television show from Hollywood. The blue moose had a lot of little gold ornaments on chains around his neck. He was wearing sunglasses, and a pink sweater.

The movie came out. Mr. Breton, Mr. Bobowicz, the game warden, and Dave, the hermit, went to see it. Dave was worried about going into the theater with so many people, because he was so shy. Mr. Breton and Mr. Bobowicz finally solved the problem by giving Dave a paper bag, with eyeholes cut out, to wear over his head. It was a good movie. The movie people had made a very realistic space moose. Robert Blueford, a famous actor, played the part of the blue moose.

Even though it was a good movie, Mr. Breton was sad when he got home. He thought that the moose would probably stay in Hollywood, writing books and movies. He thought he should probably find someone to help him in the restaurant—but he really didn't want to.

10

THE NEXT MORNING, the morning after Mr. Breton had gone to see the movie of *The True Story of a Wild Moose*, he found the blue moose in the kitchen.

"Chef," said the moose, "we appear to be very low on onions, butter, carrots, and flour. Is there anything else I should get?"

"Moose! You came back!" Mr. Breton shouted.

"Naturally," said the moose. "Did I ever say I wouldn't?"

"No, you didn't," Mr. Breton said, "but I thought you were going to live in Hollywood and be a famous writer."

"Well, I did consider it," the moose said, "but it got to be very boring. Besides, they had that fellow, Robert Blueford, play me in the movie, and they could have had me. Chef, there are very few people with really good taste in this country. That's why I'd rather stay here with you."

"Are you going to write any more books?" Mr. Breton asked.

"I don't think so," the moose said. "I thought I'd get to work on finding a cure for every disease known to Man or Moose."

"That's a very good idea," Mr. Breton said.

"It may take quite a while," said the blue moose. "I hope you don't mind if I continue to work around the restaurant while I do my research."

"Not at all," Mr. Breton said.

"Thanks, Chef," the moose said. "I'll go and get the groceries now."

MOOSE QUESTIONS AND ANTLERS

What do moose really look like?

If you have the chance to look at a moose for a long time—or a picture of a moose, should the real thing not be handy—you will notice that it is one weird-looking animal. Its front and back legs look like they are from two different animals. It has a long nose, and scruffy fur, and in general appears to have been put together from leftover parts. But, in fact, it is a wonderfully designed animal. Its large body helps the moose retain body heat.

Moose live in areas where the winters are long and cold and food becomes scarce. Large animals don't have to eat as frequently as small ones. Moose fur is made up of hollow hairs, which means it is insulated, for heat retention, and also helps the moose float better when swimming. Its long legs help the moose keep its body above snow level and out of wet and swampy places, thus saving energy and body heat. Being tall also allows the moose to reach food as much as eight feet above the ground. Its long nose warms frigid air, and also houses a highly developed smelling apparatus.

Wolves, cougars, and humans prey on moose, and the moose's sense of smell is its first defense. Its second line of defense is its long legs—moose run fast. Even the dewlap, or bell, has a function—it is used to spread scent so that other moose, usually the opposite sex, can get in touch. The skin of the moose makes good leather, and I am told moose are good to eat, but I have never tasted one.

Are there any moose in France?

Moose do not live in France. But Thomas Jefferson, when he was the American minister to France, had a complete moose skeleton, including the skin and antlers, shipped to him in Paris. He had the bones assembled in the lobby of his hotel. This was to help the French people get over their idea that animals in the New World were smaller than and inferior to those in Europe.

THE
MOOSEPIRE

THIS IS A story I was told by Sir Charles Pacamac, World's Champion Samovar Crasher. Sir Charles is a famous geographer. He had lectured at the University of London, where I met him when I was a very young man.

I was a guest of Sir Charles at his London club, the Amphibolus.

We were enjoying a cup of tea when the distinguished geographer said, "Pinkwater, you miserable half-wit, have I ever told you of my experience with the dreaded Vampire Moose of North America?"

"No, Sir Charles," I said. "In fact, I've never

heard of such a thing as a Vampire Moose. What is it?"

"I tell you, Pinky, it is a dreadful creature," Sir Charles said. "Not many men have ever seen one—and even fewer have lived to tell the tale. I encountered one in the wilds of North America a number of years ago. It was a remarkable experience—but even more remarkable was another moose I met at about the same time. This moose spoke very good English and he was as blue as . . . as . . . as an onion—ever hear of anything like that, Pinkwater, you ragamuffin?"

In fact, I had not only heard of the famous Blue Moose, but had written two books about him. However, I could not expect a distinguished person such as Sir Charles Pacamac to have any interest in my unimportant writings, so I politely asked, "Blue as an onion?"

"Well, blue as a what-do-you-call-it then. Confound it, man, the moose was blue! Blue as an asparagus! And he spoke like a gentleman—which is more than I can say for you, Pinkwater, you drooling idiot. Do you want to hear this story or not?"

"Certainly, Sir Charles," I said, sipping my cup of Lapsang Souchong and puffing my cheroot.

"Then stop that blasted sipping and puffing. You make me nervous!" said the wonderful old Englishman.

"I'd like to hear the story very much," I said.

"Very well—if you insist," said Sir Charles. "Make yourself comfortable. I'll summon the serving wallah. Yitzhak! Bring Pinkwater Bwana a baked potato! You may as well have a snack—this story will take some time."

The Pakistani waiter brought me a baked potato on a stick, and I settled back in my leather armchair, and listened to Sir Charles's remarkable account:

"I was studying a plague of gerbils in the Northern Territory. In order to be near the subject of my study, I had to put up in a primitive little town called Yellowtooth in the back of beyond. It was forty degrees below freezing in the shade, and the most congenial entertainment available to the locals was sucking on chunks of ice and then trying to whistle.

"I had taken a room at the local hotel, a vile

place called the Morpheus Arms. In the evening, I would descend to the taproom for a saucer of fermented mare's milk. There I engaged the natives in conversation. It appeared they were all afraid of some ghostly animal—a moose of tremendous size, with glowing eyes and fangs. All of them swore they had seen it—or knew someone who had. It sounded like a load of tapioca to me.

"The inhabitants of Yellowtooth called this imaginary moose Deadly Eric—or Eric the Dead. They believed he was a sort of moose zombie, a walking deadster. Eric was supposed to lie in wait for solitary travelers and then leap upon them and suck the wax out of their ears, causing them to go insane or worse. This is the sort of balderdash people always tell in remote places where there is nothing to do. I was mildly amused and did nothing to discourage this harmless belief of the simple inhabitants of Yellowtooth.

"Then, one night, I was just about to go to bed when I saw something amazing through the window. Standing in the middle of the main street of Yellowtooth, bathed in moonlight—bright as an onion—was the largest moose I had ever seen.

When I say that this moose was large, I want you to understand that all moose are large. Large might almost be a synonym for moose. This moose was gigantic! He was as big as an . . . as an . . . as an onion! This moose was as big as a big, colossal, enormous, gigantic, oversized, vast, impossible, huge onion—if you can imagine that. Well? Don't just sit there sucking on that baked potato, man! Do you understand what I'm talking about or not, you blasted nudnik?"

"The moose was as large as an onion," I said. "If an onion were to be of stupendous size."

"Yes. That's it exactly," said Sir Charles. "Now let me get on with my story. No more interruptions, please. As I said, there was this really big moose, just standing in the middle of the street. He had eyes that glowed like onions, and he had sharp fangs. I can tell you, I would rather have faced a rhino in my shorts than deal with that fellow.

"However, I pride myself on remaining cool in a crisis. I had my camera at hand—I'd been photographing the gerbils, you see—and I screwed in a flashbulb and let fly. I got three or four pictures of

the brute before he turned and sauntered out of town, just as fearless as an . . . as an . . . as an . . ."

"As an onion?" I put in.

"As an onion? That doesn't make sense at all. Are you sure you're following this story?"

I said I was.

"Then kindly don't keep breaking in with irrelevancies. Now, where was I? Oh, yes, the moose was fearless as an eggplant, and he just walked out of town. I was down to the chemist's like a shot the next morning to have my photos developed.

"The photos were remarkable. I had extra wallet-size prints made and sent them on the next dogsled to my friend, Professor Anton Wildebeeste, at the University of Saskatoon. The professor arrived in person five days later. He was very excited. 'If this is what it appears to be,' said Professor Wildebeeste, 'that is, if these photographs are really of Eric the Dead—then they prove something very important.'

" 'What is that?' I asked.

" 'They prove that he really exists! For years I too have heard the legends, but had hoped they were not true. You see, there was no evidence—no proof. Now, with these photographs, we have to assume that this monster moose is real. Do you think he is dangerous?'

" 'He looked dangerous. I had the feeling that he was dangerous. I would say, yes. Yes, he is dangerous.'

" 'I think he is dangerous too,' said Professor Wildebeeste.

" 'The local people all think he is dangerous,' I said.

" 'You didn't show them the photographs?' Professor Wildebeeste asked.

" 'No, I didn't want to frighten them,' I said.

" 'Good. That is good. They can do nothing. There is no reason to cause panic. Also, we can do nothing. There is only one person who can save civilization from this terrible Deadly Eric—and that person . . . is not . . . a . . . person.'

" 'Not a person?' I asked. 'Then what?'

" 'The only being known to me who can deal with this horrible monster moose,' said Professor Wildebeeste, 'is a moose himself.'

"I was amazed. I did not believe my ears. Surely, my old friend Professor Wildebeeste could not mean what he said.

" 'Surely you do not mean it,' I said. 'You believe that a moose is the only person to deal with this monster?'

" 'That's what I said, Sir Charles,' the professor said. 'I would like you to meet this remarkable moose. Will you come with me?'

"So the professor took me to meet this Blue Moose, and we had a chat with him. I must say that even though he was a quadruped, he had very good manners, almost as though he were an Englishman himself. Still, I had misgivings about trusting a beast with fur and antlers, but the professor assured me that the moose was all right.

" 'I will look into this matter,' the Blue Moose said.

" 'But what are you going to do?' I asked.

" 'Professor Wildebeeste knows my methods,' the moose said. 'He will explain to you that I prefer to work alone and in secret.'

" 'But can you do anything about the Vampire Moose?' I asked.

" 'That remains to be seen. First I must do some research.'

" 'But no one has ever seen Eric the Dead

before!' Professor Wildebeeste shouted. 'Where can you do research about an imaginary monster?'

" 'I'll start in the usual place,' the moose said.

" 'And where is that?'

" 'The public library, of course,' the moose said.

"I suppose the moose went to the library. I'm dashed if I know what he found out there. I never saw him or the monster again. A year or two later, Professor Wildebeeste wrote to me to say that the Blue Moose had taken care of the Deadly Eric business. Amazing, what?"

"But how did the Blue Moose deal with the monster—the Vampire Moose?" I asked Sir Charles.

"No idea, old fig—just a deuced amazing critter, that moose. Spoke as well as an Englishman—better than you, Pinky. Amazing story, what?"

"You mean you never found out exactly what happened?" I asked.

"No. I finished my work on the wild gerbils, and packed up and came back to London. I just thought you'd like to hear about the Blue Moose—unusual animal."

I knew then what I had to do. I had to find out what had happened when the Blue Moose met

Deadly Eric. I would go to Yellowtooth at once and begin tracking down the story. I made preparations to leave.

"I have to leave now, Sir Charles," I said.

"Fine, fine, young man," Sir Charles said. "Just have that hundredweight of onions delivered to my town address."

"Onions?" I asked.

"Yes. Aren't you the man from the wholesale greengrocers?"

"No, Sir Charles," I said. "I am Daniel Pinkwater, famous author and noted mooseologist."

"I never heard such rot in my life," said Sir Charles. "Just pay for your baked potato and get out of my sight."

I set fire to Sir Charles's walking stick, and left the adorable old Englishman musing over his memories in the Amphibolus Club. Later that day I left London. I took a plane. Then I took a train. . . . Then I took a bus. Then I took a dogsled. . . . Then I walked on snowshoes. In three days I was in Yellowtooth. I remembered what the Blue Moose had said about the best place to begin one's research. I went straight to the public library.

I was afraid the library might be closed, because all of the citizens appeared to be at the ice-sucking and whistling finals in the school gymnasium. However, I was in luck. The library was open and the head librarian was there. Mildred Beeswax was the head librarian, a handsome woman of eighty or ninety years of age.

"I am Daniel Pinkwater, famous author and noted mooseologist," I said.

"I know all about that," Mildred Beeswax said. "You wrote those silly books about the Blue Moose."

"Ah," I said, flattered, "then you have my books in this library?"

"No."

"Not even one?"

"No. I won't have them in my library. We have standards here."

"I see. Of course. Um. Well, in fact, it is about the Blue Moose that I have come to see you."

"I don't know why that moose doesn't sue you for defamation of character," Mildred Beeswax said. "If you ever put me in a book, sonny, you'd better put down everything I say, and make sure you get it right."

"Certainly," I said to the librarian. "So you remember the Blue Moose?"

"Of course I do, pip-squeak," Mildred Beeswax said. "What do you want to know about him?"

"I believe he came here once to do some research."

"Yes. He came here when he was called in on the case of Deadly Eric, the Vampire Moose," Mildred Beeswax said.

"That's what I want to know about," I said. "What happened then?"

"I have no idea, tubby," the librarian said. "I was out that week with the Book-mo-sled, delivering literature to the gold miners up in the hills. What a bunch of rascals! Wheee!"

"You weren't here?"

"No, goofus—my assistant, Matilda Flintwhistle, was in charge when the Blue Moose turned up. I'm sorry I missed him. On the other hand, I had a lot of fun up at the diggings."

"And where is Ms. Flintwhistle?" I asked.

"She wandered off during the thaw one year," Mildred Beeswax said. "Poor dear. I don't know what became of her."

"So I've come all the way from London, traveling by plane, train, dogsled, and snowshoes, having eaten nothing but a baked potato in the past three days, and the only person who might remember the Blue Moose's visit is gone, and you don't know *where?*"

"That's right, dope," Mildred Beeswax said. "You'd have saved some trouble if you'd telephoned from London. We answer questions by telephone, you know."

"So there's no way for me to find out what happened when the Blue Moose came here!"

"Not unless you read the manuscript he sent us."

"The moose sent you a manuscript?"

"Yes. It's sort of a diary of the case of Deadly Eric."

"And you've got it here?"

"Certainly."

"And I can see it?"

"Are your hands clean?"

"I washed them on the dogsled."

"Then yes, you may."

Mildred Beeswax led me to a table and brought me a blue notebook. It was written in longhoof.

This is what I read:

The Case of the Vampire Moose

In order to escape unwanted publicity created by the books written by that fool, Pinkwater, I was forced to move to the northernmost wilderness. Fortunately, not many copies of the books were sold, and it looked as though I would be able to return to my normal life in a short time.

I was terribly bored in the Northland. There wasn't much to do beyond sucking chunks of ice and trying to whistle. I was grateful when I received a visit from my old friend, Professor Anton Wildebeeste of the University of Saskatoon. He had with him an English naturalist, Sir Charles Pacamac, whom I remembered as the World's Champion Samovar Crasher. I was honored to meet the great athlete.

It developed that Professor Wildebeeste wanted my help in the matter of a vampire moose that had been terrorizing a small community—Yellowtooth. I promised Professor Wildebeeste that I would deal with the matter, and left for Yellowtooth at once.

Arriving in the miserable little town, I realized that I had no idea how to deal with this matter. I had never seen or heard of a vampire moose that sucked ear wax and terrorized people. In fact, with few exceptions, moose are superior animals, good members of society, and lots of fun. I spent some time in conversation with the locals, but found them to be a superstitious lot with very little solid information to share about the vampire other than his name—Deadly Eric.

I turned to my usual starting point in any research—the public library—where I found Matilda Flintwhistle, the helpful assistant librarian. Ms. Flintwhistle told me I had free run of the library. I went right to work.

My first stop was the good old card catalog. I looked up books on vampires, the history of vampires, vampire hunting, vampires in art, literature, movies, and television, and vampires named Eric. Also, in the crafts section, books on how to make a vampire out of clay, wood, and papier-mâché. I also looked up books on large land animals of North America, the natural history of the deer family (to which moose belong), famous moose in

history, a book called *Who's Moose*, a novel called *Forever Antler*, and, of course, the *Moose Scout Handbook*. I was pleased to see how many books there were about moose. I wrote down the title, author, and number of each book on a separate little piece of paper.

Some books I needed were not in the public library of Yellowtooth—for example, those awful books by that idiot, Pinkwater. To be thorough, I thought I'd better read them, so I asked Ms. Flintwhistle to order them for me on interlibrary loan.

I also asked Ms. Flintwhistle to look up the number of citizens of Yellowtooth who had gone mad in the past ten years—with special emphasis on those who had gone mad after an encounter with a supernormal moose. I also looked up books on madness, earwax, psychoneurosis, the treatment of insane people, people who have had strange experiences, and folktales about big animals who jump out of the dark at people and do nasty things to them.

Then I looked up books of geography, the history of the area around Yellowtooth, and the diaries of early settlers in the vicinity. I planned to look through these diaries for any mention of the Vampire Moose.

I also looked up books about the legends of the local Indian people for the same purpose.

In order to be prepared to deal with the Vampire Moose when I met him, I looked up books on trapping, hunting, building traps, self-defense, how to overpower huge angry animals, and first aid.

As I found the card for each book, I wrote down the number, author, and title. By this time I had filled a considerable number of little pieces of paper.

Then, in the encyclopedias and dictionaries, I looked up moose, vampires, legends, madness, trapping, fighting, moose with the name Eric, and methods for dealing with supernatural beings. I also looked at microfilms of old newspaper articles. While I was doing this, Ms. Flintwhistle was finding the books I had noted on my pieces of paper. There were 962 of them.

However, I was not yet finished. In the phonograph record department, I listened to a record of moose calls, and an opera called *Fledermoose*.

I also listened in to Ms. Flintwhistle reading a story to some children who had come to the library. The story was about a moose named Heinrich. It was nice to be read to. I sat on the floor with the children and had a pleasant time.

I then checked out the 962 books. (Ms. Flintwhistle had issued me a temporary library card.)

By this time evening was approaching, and there was to be a film shown at the library. I stayed and watched it. It was called *Mushroom Gathering in the Andes*. I had never seen it before. Amazingly, it turned out to be my lifetime favorite movie. It showed the happy people of the high mountains, going around looking for mushrooms! It was wonderful! The narration told all about mushrooms and how to find them. I made a note to come back to the library after I had dealt with the Vampire Moose, and check out some books about mushrooms, amateur mushroom growing, mushroom culture for profit, South America, the Andes Mountains, films, filmmaking, fungi, poisonous fungi, how to recognize poisonous fungi, and what to do if you accidentally eat a poisonous fungus.

I then took the 962 books to the empty boxcar on the deserted railway siding where I was staying. I could have taken a room at the Morpheus Arms, but I wanted to come and go unseen. Also, the boxcar didn't cost anything, and rooms at the Morpheus Arms cost $1.75 a day.

The first thing I did after I had settled into my boxcar with my 962 library books was to write a letter to my friend, Mr. Breton.

Mr. Breton is my employer. I help him run his restaurant. I also get to live in a room upstairs for free. I like Mr. Breton, and the restaurant, and my room. I would never have left home but for the unwanted publicity brought by the books written by that infernal Daniel Pinkwater.

The truth is, I was feeling a little homesick. This is the letter I wrote my friend and employer, Mr. Breton:

Dear Chef,
    I am solving the case of a vampire moose here in the frozen North. I have begun my research on the subject.
    I will write to you from time to time.

There may be danger, but it is my duty to do all I can to help man and moosekind.

Please say hello to Dave, the hermit, and Mr. Bobowicz, the game warden.

I wish I had a bowl of your clam chowder.

Your friend,

The Moose

The Moose

I felt a bit better after writing the letter. Then I settled down to read the books I had checked out. I had a few dozen onions for supper. There was a bright full moon, so I was able to read far into the night.

By the next morning, I had read 943 of the library books. I now knew nearly everything about vampires, vampire hunting, vampires in art, literature, movies, and television, vampires named Eric, how to make a vampire out of clay, wood, and papier-mâché, large land animals of North America, the natural history of the deer family, famous moose in history, how to tie moose knots, various statistics regarding madness and moose in

Yellowtooth, insanity, spooky animals, local history, trapping, hunting, self-defense, and how to overpower huge angry animals.

My next step was to set about capturing Eric the Dead himself. To this end, I searched the woods for signs of the Vampire Moose. I knew what to look for because I'd read the books. There was not a single sign of a vampire moose—or a vampire—or a moose (other than myself).

I took to lurking around the town of Yellowtooth, listening under windows and in public places for some mention of Deadly Eric. Nothing special. Nobody had seen the monster lately, and the conversation about him was getting stale.

There was nothing to do but wander the woods, waiting and thinking. I did so. I wandered. I thought. I studied the features of the forest—the moss, the grasses, the trees, the little woodland creatures. This was somewhat boring for me. As a moose, I already knew all about that sort of thing. But there was still no sign of the Vampire Moose, so I had nothing to do but wait.

I must admit I was getting lonely, and I was

grateful when Nathan of the North showed up. Nathan of the North was an old prospector, mountain man, trapper, scout, mule driver, hunter, and conservative Jewish rabbi. He knew a lot about life in the woods, and also Talmudic commentary. Nathan taught me the blessing for onions-and-moss soup.

Nathan asked whether he could stay with me in my boxcar. I told him I would be only too glad to have some company. He moved in with his traps and prayer books, and a chicken he'd picked up somewhere along the trail.

I asked Nathan of the North if he knew anything about the Vampire Moose.

"I'll look it up," he said.

Nathan of the North reported to me that there was nothing in any of his books of Hebrew lore and philosophy, except for a brief reference to a bagel vampire called Noshferatu.

"You know, there was nothing specific about Deadly Eric or any vampire moose in any of the stuff I took out of the library either," I said.

"Are you sure the Moosepire isn't fictional?" Nathan of the North asked me. "For it is written (somewhere), a thing isn't a thing unless it is a thing."

"Did you bring any of those Jewish crackers?" I asked Nathan.

"Matzohs, also known as matzoth?" Nathan replied. "I have some in my pack. We shall sit here in the wilderness and eat matzohs or matzoth, for it is written (but I forget where) that we shall sit in the wilderness and eat matzohs. Or matzoth."

Nathan of the North was a nice chap, and I was glad for his company—but I could see he was going to be no help at all in catching the Vampire Moose.

"Maybe you should use some sort of bait to catch him," Nathan said. "What does he like?"

"I hear he likes ear wax," I said.

"Yicch!" said Nathan of the North.

"Well, I'm going to go and look around for him one more time," I said.

"Fine," said Nathan. "I'll stay here and say my prayers and then make some birch-bark tea and fungus and lichen stew."

"Yicch!" I said.

I had looked everywhere possible for Deadly

Eric, not once but ten times. I was pretty discouraged. I decided that my best bet was to lurk in town and try to overhear things. I also liked lurking better because a town, even Yellowtooth, is more interesting to me than the great wilderness.

It may be hard to believe but a moose, large as it is, can be a very successful lurker—and I, a trained detective, can make myself almost invisible when there is need. Thus I was able to go in and out of town on many lurking forays without being seen by the local inhabitants.

I would skulk into Yellowtooth, keeping within the shadows, and making no noise. Then I would listen at keyholes and under windows trying to catch some word that would help me find Deadly Eric. I also peeked into windows whenever possible, in hope of catching a glimpse of the Vampire Moose. When there was danger of being discovered, I would freeze—become utterly motionless, and blend into the darkness.

On rare occasions, I would abandon my concealment, and speak to a responsible-looking citizen. Actually, I only did this once. A fellow was emerging from a place of entertainment, and I casually walked alongside and whispered directly in his ear, "Sir, have you any information regarding the Vampire Moose, Eric the Dead? It would be a great help to me if—"

At this point, the silly fellow gave a scream and ran off into the night, shouting nonsense about Eric. An idiot of some sort, it appeared. I abandoned my idea of getting information directly from the natives.

One night, shortly after Nathan of the North had come to stay with me, someone photographed me on one of my nightly lurks. There was a flash— then another. Someone was taking my picture with the aid of a flashbulb. I stood still. I had nothing to fear, after all—I was doing no wrong. To run away would have been to draw attention to myself. I hoped the pictures had been taken by an enterprising tourist wanting a souvenir of the Northland. In my mind I congratulated the photographer on having found a moose-subject as handsome as myself. They would be prizewinning pictures, I thought.

When I arrived back at the boxcar, I found my

friend Nathan admiring some black-and-white photographs. What a coincidence.

"These are fine pictures of you, my friend," Nathan of the North said.

"Let me see," I said. "Yes, they are rather good." For a moment I thought that somehow Nathan had gotten hold of the pictures the unknown tourist had taken that very night—but how could that have been possible? "Wait!" I said. "These are not pictures of me. These are the pictures of Deadly Eric, the Moosepire, taken by Sir Charles Pacamac, and given to me by my friend Professor Anton Wildebeeste."

"No, no!" said Nathan of the North. "My practiced trapper's and rabbi's eye is not to be deceived. These are pictures of you, Moose—I have no doubt."

I examined the pictures. "You know, they do look like me," I admitted.

"It is you," Nathan said. "It looks exactly like you. Besides, what other moose wears eyeglasses?"

"But these are pictures of the Vampire Moose!" I said. "I am confused."

"Unless . . . ," said Nathan of the North.

"Unless?" I asked, wondering.

"Unless, *you* are the Vampire Moose," Nathan of the North said.

"But how could that be?" I asked.

"Now I am confused," said Nathan of the North.

We pondered the question. We pondered for three days and three nights. At the end of that time, we still had not come up with an acceptable theory that would explain how I could be the moose in the photographs of Deadly Eric, the Vampire Moose, which Sir Charles Pacamac had taken.

We stopped pondering for a snack. Nathan of the North prepared a huge quantity of pinecone soup and Jewish crackers. I had fifteen bowls, and Nathan of the North had eleven. We ate so much that we could barely move.

Then Nathan of the North took to pacing. First he walked up and down, trying to figure out the mystery of how I could be in the photos of the Vampire Moose. Then he paced in circles. Then he paced around and around the boxcar. Then he paced through the boxcar, entering it by the door on the north end, and coming out the door on the south end.

"Aren't you getting hungry?" Nathan of the North asked. "I could eat a whole lot of pinecone soup and matzohs or matzoth right now."

"You just had eleven bowls of the stuff," I said. "How could you be hungry already?"

"Nonsense," said Nathan of the North. "I haven't eaten much of anything for the past three days while we've been trying to figure out this mystery."

"You don't remember eating?"

"I didn't eat. I'm starving. I'm empty."

"Impossible," I said.

"But true," said Nathan of the North.

"I have a sort of dim idea," I said. "Sit right there, and don't move."

I scribbled a note and tied it to my right hoof. Then I galloped through the north door of the boxcar, and came out the south door. "I'm hungry," I said.

Then I noticed the note. "What's this?" I said. I read the note:

If you don't remember having written this note, go into the door on the south side of the boxcar, and come out the door on the north side—but first, write on the bottom of the note whether you are hungry or not. This is serious. Do it!

I wrote "hungry" at the bottom of the note, and galloped into the door on the south side of the boxcar and out the door on the north side. When I came out, I remembered why I had written the note in the first place—and the word I had added at the bottom proved my theory. I burped.

"Nathan of the North, I have solved the mystery!" I said.

"I'm hungry," said Nathan of the North.

My experiment had worked. My theory was proven. The boxcar was actually some sort of time machine—and if one entered it by the north side and emerged from the south side, one would go back in time. If one entered the boxcar from the south door and came out the north door, one would go forward in time.

I remembered remarking to myself when I first found the boxcar that I had never seen any railroad equipment made out of what I took to be shiny aluminum that glowed green at night. "This boxcar is a thing from another time, or planet even," I said to Nathan of the North.

"You know, I'm going to die if I don't eat something soon," Nathan said. "How long do I have to sit here?"

"I beg your pardon," I said. "Just pass through that door, keep going, and come out the other side."

"Why?"

"Because I ask you to—and it is written in some book of wisdom or other, 'He who does not oblige his friend will get no soup.'"

Nathan did as I asked. He entered the boxcar by the door on the north side and came out of the one on the south side.

"Ready for a big meal?" I asked him.

"Are you crazy?" Nathan of the North asked me. "I'm so full of soup I'm afraid I might plotz, or explode."

"This is most remarkable," I said.

"What is?" asked Nathan of the North.

"I have figured out how it can be that I am the Vampire Moose."

"You have?"

"Yes."

"So?"

"So what?"

"So how is it possible?"

"This is how. The boxcar is a time machine."

"It is?"

"It is. You go in one door and come out the other, and you will go back and forth in time. I haven't quite figured out how to operate the thing—but we just had a demonstration."

"We did?"

"We did. You ate a lot, walked in one door and out the other, and all of a sudden you were hungry again—why?"

"Why? Tell me."

"I'll tell you. You went back in time to just before you ate."

"So I was hungry again."

"Exactly. Later, when you went through the time machine in the other direction, you went forward in time to the present—after having eaten—so you weren't hungry."

"So I wasn't hungry." Nathan of the North was

trying to take it all in. "But how does this make you Deadly Eric?"

"Somehow, I went a good deal further back in time, and turned up in Yellowtooth. Sir Charles Pacamac took some photos of me with a flashbulb. He thought I was Deadly Eric.

"When I whispered in a citizen's ear, he took it to be the Vampire Moose trying to suck the wax out of his ears, and this added to the general panic."

"So who is the real Moosepire?" Nathan of the North asked.

"You mean other than me? There is no Moosepire other than me."

"How can you be sure?" Nathan of the North asked.

"Well, I can't be one hundred percent sure," I said. "But none of my research at the public library turned up any evidence of there being a real Moosepire. The only photos of the Moosepire look just like me. We seem to have stumbled on a time machine, and . . ."

"Where do you suppose that came from?" asked Nathan of the North.

"I was wondering that myself," I said. "It may have been left here by some time traveler—or it might have gotten away from whoever owns it."

"You were saying about the Moosepire."

"You know, Nathan of the North, I am bored with the Moosepire, aren't you?"

"Well, now that we both believe it was you all the time, it is quite boring—but to tell the truth, I was bored from the beginning."

"I will send a postcard to Professor Wildebeeste, and tell him the Vampire Moose business is settled. There is no need to go into the details—it might be embarrassing. Then let's see if we can learn to work this time machine."

"Do you suppose we can get it to take us to the eighteenth century?" Nathan of the North asked. "I've always wanted to go there."

"We can see," I said. "Theoretically, it should be able to take us to any time period at all. Do you have any desire to see the distant future?"

"Can we see the eighteenth century too?"

"Why not?"

"Well, if we can go to both, I have no objection to visiting the distant future."

Nathan of the North and I began our study of the time machine. We soon had a fairly good idea of how it worked, and we prepared to become time travelers. Our first experiment was . . .

Here the manuscript abruptly ended. I asked the librarian, Mildred Beeswax, if there had been any more pages.

"That's all there is, bozo," the librarian said. "Now haul your fat little self out of here—it's closing time."

I left the library and went out into the streets of Yellowtooth. I had traveled through vast wilderness, I had been subjected to insults, and I had starved, and suffered from reader's cramp—but I had found out the true story of the Moosepire. What was more, I was now ready to write another book about the Blue Moose, and earn fame and vast sums of money by doing so.

Sucking on an icicle I had broken off the library building, I made my way to the highway, to hitch a ride on a passing dogsled.

MOOSE QUESTIONS
AND ANTLERS

Have you ever actually seen a moose?
This author was once putting gas in his car in Greenville, Maine, when a moose calmly walked through the gas station—just strolled through, among the gas pumps, and out the other side.

"Look! Look! A moose! A moose!" the excitable fat writer shouted, pointing and jumping up and down.

The old Maine type, whose gas station it was, barely looked up, and said, "Drat! When the moose start coming into town this early in the fall, it means we're going to have an early winter."

What should I call a moose if I meet one?

Female moose are called cows and usually give birth to twins, sometimes triplets. Moose calves can browse, which means to nibble plant life, and follow their mother at three weeks. They are completely weaned at five months but stay with their mother for at least a year.

Male moose are called bulls—by people. We don't know what moose call each other, but they do communicate with sounds—horrible weird-sounding sounds.

What should I do if I see a moose?

Moose have poor eyesight but good hearing and a good sense of smell. They are good swimmers and can progress at six miles an hour—for an hour. If a moose charges you—which can happen—standing still is not a good idea. It is better to run away, because moose will not chase you very far. However, they can run at speeds up to fifty-five miles per hour. So run fast. Really fast.

The moose is blue,
Your wish will come true.

• • • • •

ABOUT THE AUTHOR

The *Washington Post* wrote that Daniel Pinkwater is a national treasure. He started writing books for children and young readers in 1969. He likes to write for kids because they are such attentive readers and they cannot be fooled. Pinkwater's *Lizard Music* and *Blue Moose* (the latter included in this volume) are considered classics of children's literature. Educated as an artist, Pinkwater has been a warehouse worker, a dog trainer, a teacher, and an illustrator. His commentaries have been aired on National Public Radio since 1987. Well known as a sportsman and patron of the arts, Pinkwater owns the world's largest collection of false noses, and frequently wears one. He lives with his wife, the beautiful red-haired author and illustrator Jill Pinkwater, in a two-hundred-year-old farmhouse in New York's Hudson River valley.